D0016560

HAPPY EASTER
From The CRAYONS

HAPPY EASTER
From The CRAYONS

PHILOMEL

The crayons are
getting ready for
Easter.

Red crayon
decorates a circle.

That is NOT an EGG.
ARE YOU...
gONNa COlo
an EGG?

Orange crayon
decorates a square.

No, but IT is The COLOR OF THE SUN.

Yellow crayon decorates a triangle.

That is totally NOT an EGG.

No, but IT is The COLOR OF THE SUN.

Esteban
decorates a rectangle.

That is DEFINITELY
NOT an EGG.

White crayon
decorates a star.

That's not an EGG...
also... DID YoU even
CoLoR it ?

YES I COLORED IT
THANK you VERY MUCH!

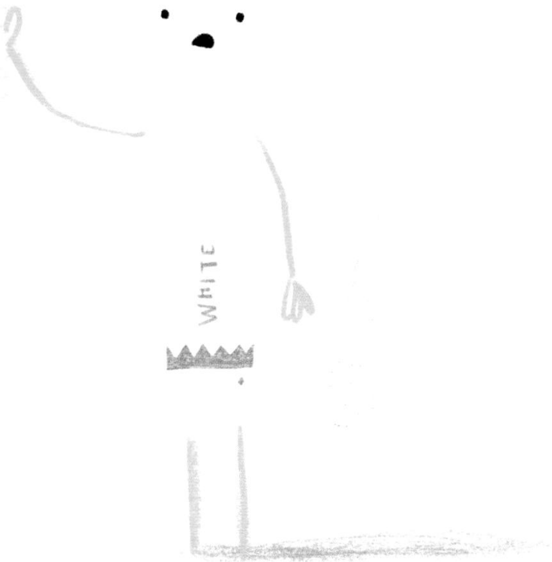

Blue crayon
decorates a rhombus.

I KNOW. NOT an EGG.
DON'T START WITH ME,
PURPLE. I NEED A nap.

Purple crayon
is super confused.

NO one is decorating
an egg!

Oh NOW I get it!
HMMM. but WHERE Are we gonNa HIDE This Thing?
Ooh, ooh, I know!
PURPLE
RED
BLUE

Philomel Books
An imprint of Penguin Random House LLC, New York

First published in the United States of America by Philomel Books,
an imprint of Penguin Random House LLC, 2023

Text copyright © 2023 by Drew Daywalt
Illustrations copyright © 2023 by Oliver Jeffers

Penguin supports copyright. Copyright fuels creativity, encourages diverse
voices, promotes free speech, and creates a vibrant culture. Thank you
for buying an authorized edition of this book and for complying with
copyright laws by not reproducing, scanning, or distributing any part of it
in any form without permission. You are supporting writers and allowing
Penguin to continue to publish books for every reader.

Philomel Books is a registered trademark of
Penguin Random House LLC.

Visit us online at penguinrandomhouse.com.

Library of Congress Cataloging-in-Publication Data is available.

Manufactured in Italy

ISBN 9780593621059

10 9 8 7 6 5 4 3 2 1

LEG

Edited by Jill Santopolo
Design by Rory Jeffers

Text set in Mercury.
Art was created with gouache, ink, colored pencil, and crayon.

The publisher does not have any control over and does not assume
any responsibility for author or third-party websites or their content.